101 USES

FOR A

DEAD IRS AGENT

By
Jim Waltz and Don Hipschman

Illustrations by
Tom Peacock

This book is sold with the understanding that the subject
matter covered herein is of a general nature and does not
constitute legal, accounting or other professional advice for
any specific individual or situation. Anyone planning to
take action in any of the areas that this book describes
should, of course, seek professional advice from accoun-
tants, lawyers, tax and other advisers, as would be prudent
and advisable under their given circumstances.

R&E Publishers
P.O. Box 2008, Saratoga, CA 95070
Tel: (408) 866-6303   Fax: (408) 866-0825

Book Cover by Kaye Quinn
Illustrations by Tom Peacock
Typesetting by elletro Productions

ISBN 0-88247-975-10

Designed, typeset and totally manufactured in the
United States of America

DEAD-ICATION

To the Internal Revenue Service and all its agents, without whom this book would not have been possible.

Readers are invited to tell us of their experiences with the IRS. Responses will be welcomed as the basis of a new book of real-life experiences which we anticipate may be even scarier than those in this book.

PAPERWORK REDUCTION ACT NOTICE

The time needed to complete and digest this book will vary depending on individual comprehension levels, prior experiences with the IRS, and whether or not the book is sitting on the back of the toilet. Our estimated times are:

Reading the joke .... 10 seconds

Understanding the joke .... 5 seconds

Copying the joke,
telling friends,
and enclosing
your favorite item
with your tax forms .... 30 seconds

Responding to the
anticipated retaliatory
audit from the IRS .... 120 hours

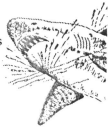

INTRODUCTION

"To tax and to please, no more than to love and be wise,
is not given to men"

EDMUND BURKE

"Taxation without representation is a tyranny."

JAMES OTIS

Taxation with representation is also a tyranny."

J.R. WALTZ

"The schoolboy whips his taxed top—the beardless youth manages
his taxed horse, with a taxed bridle, on a taxed road;—and the
dying Englishman, pouring his medicine, which has paid seven
percent, into a spoon which has paid fifteen percent—flings himself
back upon his chintz bed, which has paid twenty-two percent—and
expires into the arms of an apothecary who has paid a license of a
hundred pounds for the privilege of putting him to death."

REV. SIDNEY SMITH

"And it came to pass in those days, that there went out a decree
form Caesar Augustus, that all the world should be taxed."

ST. LUKE, Ch. 2, Verse 1, New Testament, THE BIBLE

"But in this world nothing can be said to be certain, except death
and taxes."

BENJAMIN FRANKLIN

"Neither will it be, that a people overlaid with taxes ever should
become valiant and martial."

FRANCIS BACON

"Horseness is the whatness of all-horse."

JAMES JOYCE

The "IRS-Ness" of an IRS Agent is commonly perceived as:
Humorless • Pitiless • Relentless • Shrewd • Wickedly intelligent.

GENERAL TAXPAYER INFORMATION ON HOW TO READ THIS BOOK

1. Purpose

To qualify to read *101 Uses for a Dead IRS Agent* (ISBN 0-394-50622-9), on the 15th day following the third month of each calendar year, you must qualify as a U.S. Taxpayer. See publication 17, DO I HAVE TO FILE A RETURN? IRC S6012 (a) (1) and Regs 1.60120 -1 to -6 inclusive. Exceptions — If not a Taxpayer per Code or Regulations cited, others may read this book provided it is used in an educational context to remind them to: 1.) Remain in hiding; 2.) Remain employed in any criminal enterprise unknown to the Internal Revenue Service; 3.) remain employed in any criminal enterprises known to the general public which come under the headings of (3a) Member of the House Ways and Means Committee or Senate Finance Committee, or (3b) Incumbent seeking re-election.

2. Utility

Detailed explanations are generally unnecessary, unless you wish to append specific explanations to any form you send to an IRS agent in order to comprehend the meaning. *Extreme* care in this activity is advised: see IRC S7606 (ENTRY OF PREMISES), IRC S7608, (AUTHORITY OF OFFICERS) which empowers illiterate college graduates to enter residential or other promises without a search warrant. Further, guilty readers are allowed retention of few basic necessities for living unless exchanged for unlimited interference in their lives and those of their families, and then provided that timely reports and payments are submitted. Exemptions - None from collection activity. Please note that being merely not liable for a tax in no way exempts a taxpayer from being subject to collection attempts. Best efforts, indignities, and expenses are not allowances or deductions, nor is the right to invoke Amendment XIII to the United States Constitution (adopted December 18, 1865) prohibiting slavery or involuntary servitude or Amendment XIV (adopted July 28, 1968) which forbids depriving any citizen of life, liberty, or property without due process of law.

3. Taxpayer Identification Number

When forwarding your personal experiences or anecdotes with the Internal Revenue Service to the authors care of R&E Publishers, do not include your name, address, or TIN, since anything you send may be discovered in the author's anticipated audits.

4. Disavowal

Any depiction or representation of any living IRS agent is purely coincidental and inadvertent, but well deserved.

5. Remedy

Leave the country, but remember that expenses for travel, accommodations, food, entertainment, and attendant gratuities to escape to nations such as Brazil and Libya which do not have extradition treaties with the United States may not be used as tax deductions upon subsequent reentry, whether voluntary or otherwise; See Code Section 62, or *United States of America v. Noriega.*

SCHEDULES A&B
(Form 1040)

Schedule A—Itemized Deductions

(Schedule B is on back)

OMB No. 1545-0074

1991

Department of the Treasury
Internal Revenue Service   (R)   ► Attach to Form 1040. ► See Instructions for Schedules A and B (Form 1040).

Attachment
Sequence No. 07

Name(s) shown on Form 1040

Your social security number

Medical and Dental Expenses		Caution: *Do not include expenses reimbursed or paid by others.*		
	1	Medical and dental expenses. (See page 38.)	1	
	2	Enter amount from Form 1040, line 32 [2]		
	3	Multiply line 2 above by 7.5% (.075)	3	
	4	Subtract line 3 from line 1. Enter the result. If less than zero, enter -0- ►	4	
Taxes You Paid (See page 38.)	5	State and local income taxes	5	
	6	Real estate taxes	6	
	7	Other taxes. (List—include personal property taxes.) ►	7	
	8	Add lines 5 through 7. Enter the total ►	8	
Interest You Paid (See page 39.)	9a	Home mortgage interest and points reported to you on Form 1098	9a	
	b	Home mortgage interest not reported to you on Form 1098. (If paid to an individual, show that person's name and address.) ►		
			9b	
	10	Points not reported to you on Form 1098. (See instructions for special rules.)	10	
	11	Investment interest (attach Form 4952 if required). (See page 40.)	11	
	12	Add lines 9a through 11. Enter the total ►	12	

Have a few of them enshrined at Red Cross chapters to let them know what professional blood-sucking is all about.

To poison competitors' dog sled teams in the Iditerod.

Put them through a trash compactor and pave your patio
to last as long as the 2,000 year-old Appian Way.

Use their skins for 300,000-mile guaranteed tires.

SCHEDULE SE
(Form 1040)

Department of the Treasury
Internal Revenue Service (0)

Self-Employment Tax

► See Instructions for Schedule SE (Form 1040).

► Attach to Form 1040.

OMB No. 1545-0074

1991

Attachment
Sequence No. 17

Name of person with self-employment income (as shown on Form 1040)

Social security number of person
with self-employment income ►

Who Must File Schedule SE

You must file Schedule SE if:

* Your net earnings from self-employment from other than church employee income (line 4 of Short Schedule SE or line 4c of Long Schedule SE) were $400 or more; OR
* You had church employee income (as defined in the instructions) of $108.28 or more.

Use their hearts to cut diamonds.

To train Dobermans and pit bulls.

Put their hearts on the North Pole and triple the size
of the ice cap.

Put them behind racing greyhounds to drive the dogs
to new speed records.

Make a corduroy highway out of them to test the
durability of tank treads.

Lay them end-to-end 15 layers deep to make
the Great Wall of Indiana.

Lay them side-by-side 50 layers deep across Mexico,
New Mexico, Oklahoma, Arkansas, and Louisiana
borders to keep Texans from emigrating.

Keep a reserve on hand to plug leaking dikes.

Send them to Iraq for analysis so Saddam Hussein can discover
the secrets of being a professional terrorist.

Market their hearts for paperweights in hurricane
and typhoon areas.

Slice as a substitute for clay pigeons.

Keep one of them in your closet so your air freshener
has something to do while your shoes and shorts
are with you at work.

Grind them up for gravel for Interstate highways.

Lay one on the prairie and give a vulture something fun to work on.

Sell to beer-drinking gardeners to conserve slug bait.

Give some electrical charges and let Frankenstein's monster have some real competition.

Put them in polyester suits and gold chains
and make them realtors, used car salesmen,
and television evangelists.

Use as a 5-stroke hazard on a golf course.

Send one to General Motors to improve the quality
of GMC board chairmen.

Put them in front of the monitors at NFL football games
to speed up instant replay calls.

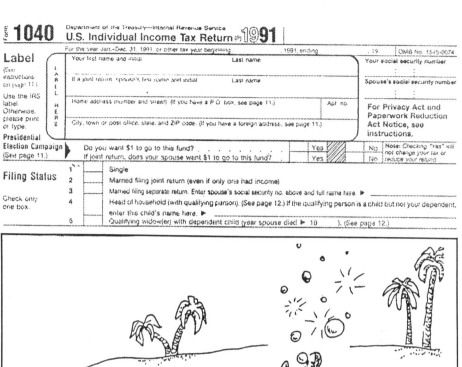
Give a crocodile indigestion.

25

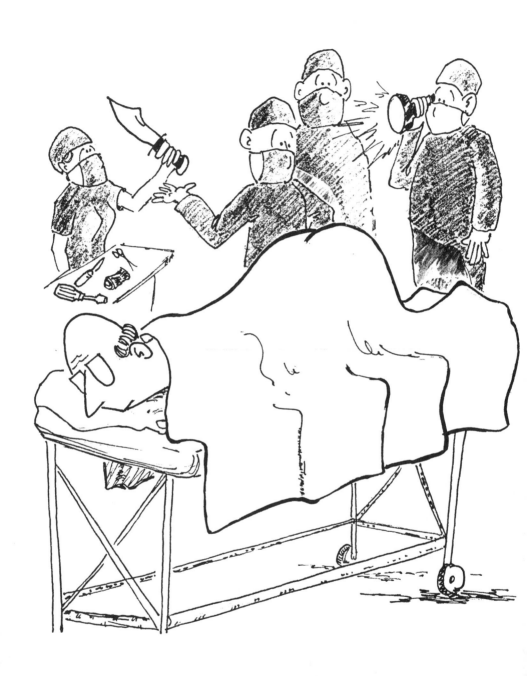

Use them for medical experiments involving
hemorrhoid transplants.

Sell them to the NFL as cheap, indestructible
tackling dummies.

Put one in every kennel and stable so no one cheats
on stud fees or just does it for fun.

To show Spock someone he wouldn't wish to
"Live long and prosper."

Use them to replace pine trees as 150-yard
golf course markers.

To test the longevity of the athlete's foot fungus.

Use them to prove there's something that Mother Theresa
wouldn't touch with a barge pole.

Use royalties from the *Dead IRS Agent's Guaranteed No-Gain Diet* to benefit the Dead IRS Agents' League.

Flatten them to line the bottoms of bird cages.

Profit or Loss From Farming

▶ Attach to Form 1040, Form 1041, or Form 1065.

▶ See Instructions for Schedule F (Form 1040).

OMB No. 1545-0074

1991

Attachment
Sequence No. 14

Name of proprietor

Social security number (SSN)

A Principal product (Describe in one or two words your principal crop or activity for the current tax year.)

B Enter principal agricultural activity code (from page 2) ▶

D Employer ID number (Not SSN)

C Accounting method   (1) ☐ Cash   (2) ☐ Accrual

E Did you make an election in a prior year to include Commodity Credit Corporation loan proceeds as income in that year? ☐ Yes ☐ No

F Did you "materially participate" in the operation of this business during 1991? (If "No," see instructions for limitations on losses.) ☐ Yes ☐ No

G Do you elect, or did you previously elect, to currently deduct certain preproductive period expenses? (See instructions.) ☐ Does not apply ☐ Yes ☐ No

Part I Farm Income—Cash Method—Complete Parts I and II (Accrual method taxpayers complete Parts II and III, and line 11 of Part I.)

Do not include sales of livestock held for draft, breeding, sport, or dairy purposes; report these sales on Form 4797.

1	Sales of livestock and other items you bought for resale	1		
2	Cost or other basis of livestock and other items reported on line 1	2		
3	Subtract line 2 from line 1			3
4	Sales of livestock, produce, grains, and other products you raised			4
5a	Total cooperative distributions (Forms(s) 1099-PATR)	5a		5b Taxable amount	5b

Wire one for each cemetery to see if anyone there figured out how to take it with them.

Sell them as friends to Al Davis, Donald Trump,
Saddam Hussein, and members of Congress.

Have at least two of them offstage at all times to remind
Madonna not to use a Form 1040 for her shorts or bra.

Sell them to barber colleges so students can practice
the loop-the-strands-across-the-bald-spot technique
of hair styling.

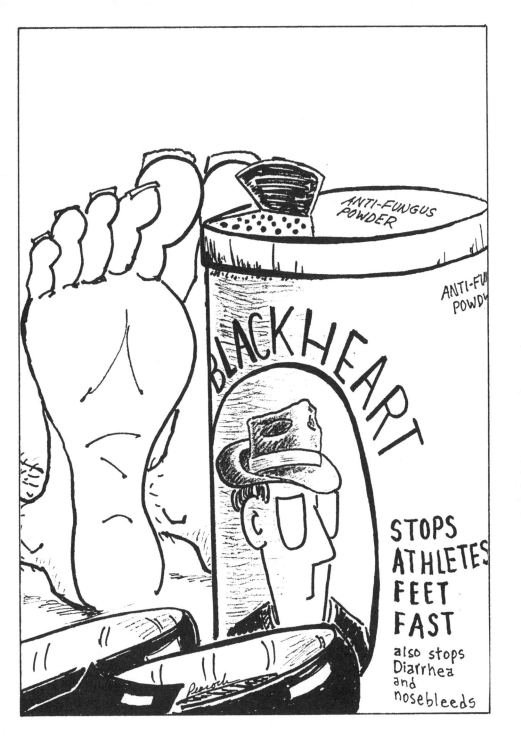

Grind up their hearts and sprinkle them inside your shoes
so that you can kill your athlete's foot fungus.

Get 200,000 or 300,000 of them for the cast of a horror
movie to be called "Midnight of April 15th!"

Sell one to each H&R Block tax office for sidewalk
displays of terror advertising.

Install them in Constipation Clinics to scare the crap
out of customers.

After your second child, put one in the middle of your living room floor as a contraceptive.

Substitute for dead chickens in hypersonic jet aircraft
windshield tents.

Before your first child, put one in the back seat of your car as a contraceptive.

After your fourth child, put one in the back seat of your secretary's car as a contraceptive.

Set one alongside each kid's lemonade stand to remind the little bastards they aren't immune from paying taxes.

Use as a substitute for coyote repellent.

Keep one in your attic to drive bats and vampires away.

Put one on your wind vane so you can explain why
misfortune is blowing from every direction.

Drop about 50,000 of them in Lake Erie as a good
beginning to test whether they remove toxins as well
as they did money.

Put some in front of each bar and liquor store
and cure alcoholism.

Let one go with Oral Roberts to see he doesn't take anything with him if the Lord calls him home because he didn't raise another $8 million.

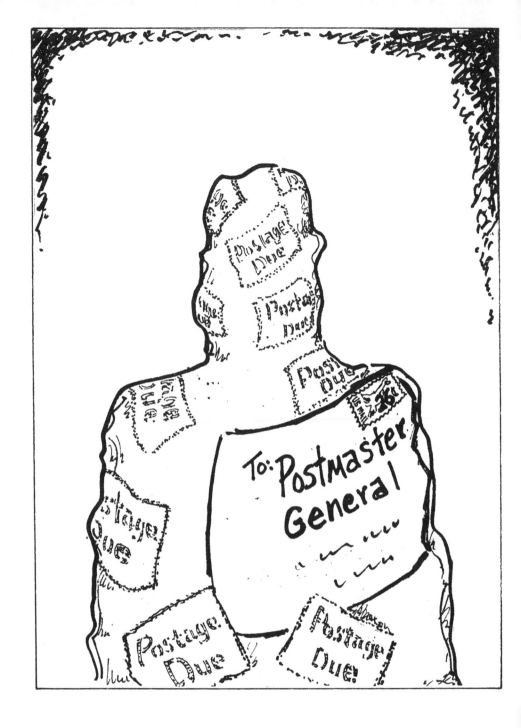

Send one postage-due to the Postmaster General
in honor of the 29-cent stamp.
(26 cents is for storage charges, you know)

Stand as an example of something no decent
environmentalist would recycle.

Put one in each "Doggie Dooley" to make sure that your dog is not withholding improperly.

Stack four or five or six on top of each other to keep
the ugly totem pole tradition alive.

In the event of a tree shortage, stand one on each block
where dogs are walked.

Schedule R
(Form 1040)

Department of the Treasury
Internal Revenue Service (P)

Credit for the Elderly or the Disabled

➤ Attach to Form 1040. ➤ See separate instructions for Schedule R.

OMB No. 1545-0074

1991

Attachment
Sequence No. 16

Name(s) shown on Form 1040

Your social security number

You may be able to use Schedule R to reduce your tax if by the end of 1991:

* You were age 65 or older, OR ● You were under age 65, you retired on permanent and total disability, and you received taxable disability income.

But you must also meet other tests. See the separate instructions for Schedule R.

Note: *In most cases, the IRS can figure the credit for you. See page 24 of the Form 1040 instructions.*

Part I Check the Box for Your Filing Status and Age

If your filing status is:	And by the end of 1991:	Check only one box
Single, Head of household, or Qualifying widow(er) with dependent child	1 You were 65 or older	1 ☐
	2 You were under 65 and you retired on permanent and total disability .	2 ☐
	3 Both spouses were 65 or older	3 ☐

Prove there's someone John McEnroe wouldn't argue with.

The ideal gift for mother-in-law's day.

Hang one beneath your sailboat for ballast.

Put a couple in the cell with Manuel Noriega so when he confesses where he hid the money the CIA paid him, we can reduce the national debt.

Trade any leftovers to Fidel Castro for one good cigar.

Use them as training dummies to teach grizzly bears
how to fetch. Then take your grizzly and go hunting
for live ones.

Fill a stadium with 200,000 Willie Nelson look-alikes
and see if even a dead IRS Agent can't spot the real
Willie Nelson.

Put one in the office of each member of Congress to remind them that PAC contributions really shouldn't go for girls, boys, booze, nose candy, hunting lodges, shares of stock in companies with government contracts, or—above all—reelection funds.

Two dead IRS agents can be used in the back of your station wagon or pickup in winter "ballasts" to save buying $1.50 sacks of sand.

A dead IRS agent can be your "responsible party"
for payroll withholding situations.

Schedule 2   Department of the Treasury—Internal Revenue Service
(Form 1040A)   **Child and Dependent Care**
    Expenses for Form 1040A Filers   **1991**   OMB No. 1545-0085

Name(s) shown on Form 1040A   Your social security number

- If you are claiming the child and dependent care credit, complete Parts I and II below. But if you received employer-provided dependent care benefits, first complete Part III on the back.
- If you are not claiming the credit but you received employer-provided dependent care benefits, only complete Part I below and Part III on the back.

Caution: *If you have a child who was born in 1991 and the amount on Form 1040A, line 17, is less than $21,250, see page 51 of the instructions before completing this schedule.*

Part I		(a) Name	(b) Address (number, street, apt. no., city, state, and ZIP code)	(c) Identifying number (SSN or EIN)	(d) Amount paid (see instructions)
Persons or organizations who provided the care	1				

After your third child, put one in the middle of your bed as a contraceptive.

Use as a real dummy for bridge.

Use as fertilizer when growing ulcer-causing plants.

Put a couple in the front seat of a roller coaster ride
and scare people on the ground, too.

Use two at the annual company picnic
for the horseshoe pits.

To train new IRS agents in the fine art
of personal interaction.

To substitute as a virgin at a Satanic Black Mass when it
calls for something really cold.

To remind you why not to have kids.

To show there are some 7-footers who won't make
the NBA player draft.

As a means of testing deodorants suspected
of causing leprosy.

Use them for a "Have a Really Rotten Day" campaign.

★ IRS AGENTS ★
MAY HAVE MOTHERS

NATIONAL INQUIRY

APRIL 15, 1992

DEVICES I HAVE USED ON TAXPAYERS

TORTURE TEC'

ACCESSING CHILDREN'S BANK ACCOUNTS

As someone who won't sue *The National Enquirer*
(but may just confiscate the whole damn thing).

For mudslide barriers in California.

To save wear and tear on your toilet plunger.

As crossbeams and bracebeams for coal mines.

The kind of scarecrow that would have caused a major plot change in "The Wizard of Oz."

As a tool to swat miller moths.

As a cutter tip on a roto-rooter.

As the only person willing to be a "best man"
at a wedding of IRS agents.

As trophies for Posse Comitatus tax-refusal tournaments.

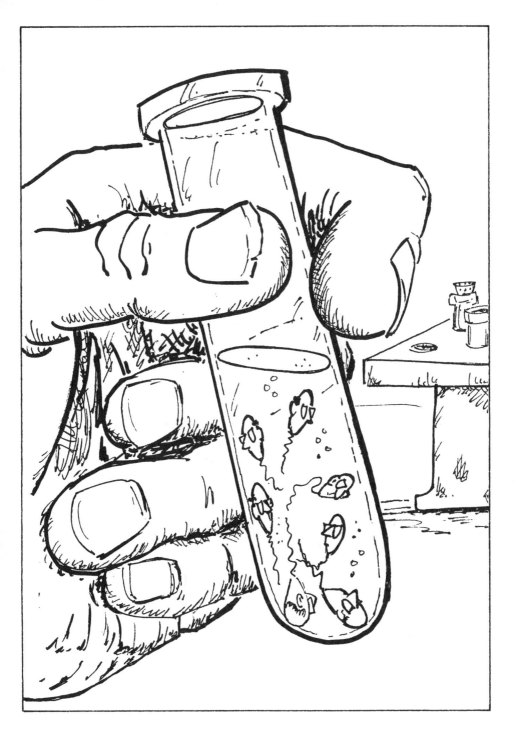

An example of what bio-technology might unleash
if it isn't watched carefully.

To teach Olympic hopefuls not to hit the slalom poles
because the $5,000 penalty plus interest really
slows them down.

Put one in your living room in case you can't afford to have your cat declawed.

To demonstrate to the Tin Man that he wouldn't need a
heart if he picked the right career.

To use as a cure for a necrophiliac.
(the corpse that even Jeffrey Dahmer couldn't love)

To keep in the bottom of aquaria to gauge the depth
of fish mulm.

An example of someone who couldn't replace Vanna
White even though the personalities are very alike.

As a tasteless substitute for tasteless dead cat
and dead lawyer jokes.

To keep Ted Turner alert to new enterprises providing
big deductions and write-offs.

To provide low-cost keynote speakers
at coroners' conventions.

Troll them through swimming and game fish areas
to scare sharks away.

Make fun of them if you dare but remember
the real power in this country is a monumentally
hard-nosed outfit.

Form **8824**

Department of the Treasury
Internal Revenue Service

Like-Kind Exchanges
(and nonrecognition of gain from conflict-of-interest sales)
➤ See separate instructions.   ➤ Attach to your tax return.
➤ Use a separate form for each like-kind exchange.

OMB No. 1545-1190

1991

Attachment
Sequence No. 49

Name(s) shown on tax return

Identifying number

Part I   Information on the Like-Kind Exchange

Note: If the property described on line 1 or line 2 is real property located outside the United States, indicate the country.

1   Description of like-kind property given up ➤ ....

2   Description of like-kind property received ➤ ....

3   Date like-kind property given up was originally acquired (month, day, year) . . . . . . | 3 | /   /
4   Date you actually transferred your property to other party (month, day, year) . . . . | 4 | /   /
5   Date the like-kind property you received was identified (month, day, year). See instructions | 5 | /   /
6   Date you actually received the like-kind property from other party (month, day, year) . | 6 | /   /

Give one to Zsa-Zsa Gabor so when whe wants to hit something
official, it doesn't have to be a cop.

101

HAVE SOME FUN...

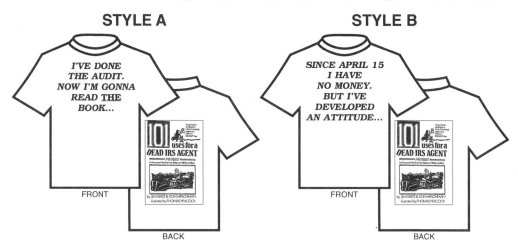

STYLE A

I'VE DONE
THE AUDIT.
NOW I'M GONNA
READ THE
BOOK...

FRONT

BACK

STYLE B

SINCE APRIL 15
I HAVE
NO MONEY.
BUT I'VE
DEVELOPED
AN ATTITUDE...

FRONT

BACK

ATTENTION-GETTING T-SHIRTS

The tradition of having fun aggravating the tax collector goes back more than 4,000 years to the Egyptian Dynasties. Here's the most contemporary expression of letting the world know what you think about taxes and the people who collect them.

SEND COPIES TO
YOUR FRIENDS, YOUR CPA
...makes a great gag gift

Available now at your favorite book store. Here's the ideal gift for those fortunate friends of yours who are forever bewailing the amount of taxes they must pay...for your CPA, tax attorney, or accountant who suffer through April 15 with you...and for people like Leona Helmsley who didn't think it could happen to them! (If you received this as a gift and aren't near a good bookstore, use the form at right to order by mail.)

Only $10.40
(What else?)

See book order blank to order

and make a statement!

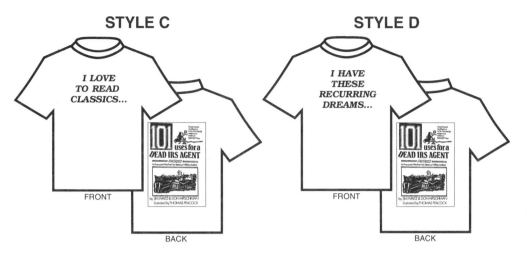

STYLE C

I LOVE
TO READ
CLASSICS...

FRONT

BACK

STYLE D

I HAVE
THESE
RECURRING
DREAMS...

FRONT

BACK

Only $14.95 Each, 2 for $25.00, 3 for $35.00

Share the fun with your friends, your accountant or CPA...and even your IRS agent (They're really human, too, you know). Available in S, M, L, and XL in a durable and comfortable cotton-poly blend. Prices include shipping and handling.

SEND YOUR ORDER TODAY!

RC Fulfillment Services, 4950 S. Yosemite, F-2, Suite 17, Englewood, CO 80111

Yes! Send the following items:

STYLE	SIZE	QTY.	EACH	PRICE
A	S,M,L,XL	_____	_____	$ _____
B	S,M,L,XL	_____	_____	$ _____
C	S,M,L,XL	_____	_____	$ _____
D	S,M,L,XL	_____	_____	$ _____

Order book from "book order blank"

Colorado Residents add Sales Tax $ _____

Allow 4-6 weeks for delivery   **TOTAL** $ _____

Make checks or money order payable to RC Fulfillment.

Bill my: ☐ VISA ☐ MasterCard.   Exp. _____

Card # ☐☐☐☐☐☐☐☐☐☐☐☐☐☐☐☐

Signature _____

Name Address _____

City _____ State _____ Zip _____